Breakout!

May the Guiding Paw be with you!

Hodder
Children's
Books

First published in Great Britain in 2002
by Hodder Children's Books

A Catalogue record for this book is available from the
British Library

ISBN 0 340 81757 7

Printed and bound by Bookmarque

The paper and board used in this paperback by Hodder Children's
Books are natural recyclable products made from wood grown in
sustainable forests. The manufacturing processes conform to the
environmental regulations of the country of origin.

Hodder Children's Books
a division of Hodder Headline Limited
338 Euston Road
London NW1 3BH

Chapter 1

"This is so unfair! We're innocent!"
shouted Onlee One.

The Guards laughed.

Hah!
That's what they all
say. Don't you worry,
there'll be plenty of time
to complain where
you're going!

Using electric shock-prods, the guards jabbed Onlee One and his two best friends, Chin Chee and Hammee.

Dzzzzzt!

The current made the three Muss feel
woozy and helpless.

Next they were thrown on board a prison ship. The door slammmed shut behind them as the engines roared into life.

There was only one place they could be bound ... Pen. The prison planet where all criminal Muss were sent. Onlee One and his friends were in despair. How had they ever got into this awful mess?

Chapter 2

Meanwhile, elsewhere in space, Dark Claw watched a video report from one of his Seekahs and smiled.

The robot Seekahs had hidden small spy cameras all over the Planet Muss. These sent information back to Dark Claw's secret space station, Dark Moon.

Although Dark Claw hated *all* Muss, he particularly hated Onlee One, who had spoiled his plans once too often. Now Dark Claw wanted revenge.

When the three young Muss had been accused of spying by Chancellor Brandling, Dark Claw had watched their trial with interest. They were innocent, but how could they prove it?

He chuckled now as he watched Onlee One and his friends being prodded on to the prison ship.

"At last," hissed Dark Claw.

I have him where I want him.

He turned to Ratuschka, leader of the Pi-rat gang that did all his dirty work. He handed her a gold disk.

The disk was a radio passport. Chancellor Brandling had given it to Ratuschka. Because of the radio signal it gave out, it meant she would not be stopped by Muss patrol ships.

"This is the key," Dark Claw chuckled. "You know what to do?"

Ratuschka smiled. She too had a score to settle with Onlee One.

Oh yes, Dark Claw, you can trust me. I know what to do!

Chapter 3

Planet Pen is a drab place. Its sky is brown, the ground is brown, the few bits of trees and grass are brown.

On Pen, the guards – and the spaceport – are locked inside a place called Freetown. A high electric fence surrounds them.

All Pen prisoners live outside the fence, locked away from the spaceport, which is the only way to get off the planet.

The prisoners run everything themselves. The guards are only there to stop them from escaping.

Onlee One, Chin Chee and Hammee were marched to the gates of Freetown and pushed into the wild and lonely *outside*.

A thin, sly-looking muss lay on on the ground near the gate, chewing a piece of grass. He opened one eye and glanced at the three new prisoners.

Very slowly, he got to his feet and began to walk away. He beckoned for them to follow.

Twenty minutes later, they arrived at a strange makeshift town, where the buildings seemed to be made out of anything that came to hand.

There were huts made from flattened tin cans or cardboard. There were also homes made from old prison vans.

Their guide took the three Muss to the largest building, which seemed to be made mostly from old packing cases.

Inside, a large ugly-looking Muss sat at one end of the room. Some mean-looking Muss hung around him.

"That's Bono," said the guide. "Be nice to him. He's the king round here."
Then, with a lazy wave of his paw, the guide slid away and out of the room.

Chapter 4

"So! Here are the spies!" bellowed
Bono.

Hammee was just about to protest that they were not spies, that it was all very unfair and that he was very hungry, when he felt a sharp dig in the ribs from Onlee One.

"Quiet! Don't say a word," Onlee One hissed.

Through large, dark glasses, Bono
examined the trio one at a time

"Round here, you do what I tell you.
I'm the boss...understand?"

The three friends muttered.

Bono yelled in their faces.

UNDERSTAND?!

"Yes, sir!" they shouted back.

Bono eyes creased into slits.
"That's better. Now, you'd better get
to work." He turned to two of his
Muss gang.

Take them to
the treadmills!

Chapter 5

The treadmills were large metal drums which provided electricity for the prison camp. Prisoners walked inside them to turn them round and power the generator.

It was exhausting. After a week of walking, Onlee One reckoned he must have trodden hundreds of miles inside the treadmills.

All the walking gave Onlee One time to think – to try and make sense of what had happened to him and his friends.

"Something must have happened a long time ago, between Brandling and my father, Pale One," he thought.

Now that Brandling knows who I am, she wants me out of the way.

Round and round went the wheel, day in, day out. As he walked, Onlee One looked at the old wheels and bits of machinery that lay scattered around the treadmills. Slowly an idea floated into his mind . . .

The treadmills could be Road Ragers, like the one he had raced on the planet Muss Vegas.

Onlee One took his friends to the dump during their meal break.

"Here," he said, "give us a hand lifting up this old wheel."

The power gears were broken, but the rest of the wheel was fine. Onlee One got inside and started to rock it back and forth.

He soon managed to get the wheel rolling. He held onto the central axel and used his feet to keep the wheel turning.

Chin Chee and Hammee ran alongside
as the huge wheel picked up speed.

"Hey!" they shouted.

You're Road Raging!

A crowd gathered round Onlee One. Everyone cheered as the wheel clattered across the ground, a trail of dust flying behind it.

When Onlee One returned, Bono was waiting. His lip curled. He was almost smiling!

"This looks fun!" he bellowed. "I'll find someone to race against you. If you win, I'll take you off the treadmills."

"It's a deal," said Onlee One.

Chapter 6

Later that day two wheels were made ready for the race.

Bono's rider, Lymee, was big and strong. "You can beat him," said Chin Chee. "He may be big but you are nimble."

"Please win!" whined Hammee. "I'm fed up with treadmilling!"

The race was hard. Lymee was easing into the lead when some rocket engines roared over their heads.

Zzz-wish!

"Don't look up!" Onlee One told himself.

Concentrate on the race. It's only a new batch of prisoners being delivered to this terrible planet.

But Lymee did look up. He lost his balance for a moment, tripped and was flung around inside the wheel. By the time he'd steadied himself, Onlee One had streaked ahead.

Onlee One was on a roll. He needed to win this race. Lymee was strong and was catching up, but not quickly enough.

Onlee One cruised over the winning line and whooped.

For a few minutes he'd forgotten all about his problems. For a few minutes he'd actually been having fun!

The crowd surged towards him, cheering and clapping, then it parted to let Bono through.

Well done lad! That was good sport, and we all need that to keep our spirits up here. I'll see about finding some easier work for you and your friends.

Hammee and Chin Chee jumped on top of Onlee One.

"You were brilliant!" they shouted.

But their cheers were drowned out by a loud siren. Then a harsh voice hailed them from a hover patrol.

Onlee One, lie down on the ground. Everyone else move away.

The hover patrol bristled with lasers.
Onlee One did as he was told.
A guard leaped out of the patrol
and handcuffed him.

Before he knew what was happening,
Onlee One was in the hover patrol and
zooming towards Freetown.
He couldn't even wave goodbye.

Chapter 7

Onlee One couldn't believe his eyes.

"Chancellor Brandling!"

Brandling held her arms out wide.

Dear boy!
There's been an awful
mistake. I've come to
take you home.

Onlee One let out a deep sigh. At last, the truth was out and the nightmare was over.

"But what about my friends?" he asked.

"Don't worry," Brandling assured him. "We'll get them out as soon as we can."

Brandling signed a few papers and led Onlee One to the spaceport. She pointed to a boarding ramp.

"After you," she said. "I'm sure you're keen to get away from here."

As Onlee One walked up the ramp, he began to feel uneasy. His sensitive nose smelled Rat!

As soon as he entered the spaceship, he recognised it.

"This is Ratuschka's ship!" he gasped.

He spun round. Brandling was still at the bottom of the ramp. Suddenly, from out of the shadows, two large rats grabbed him.

The spaceship doors closed. Onlee One could just see Brandling waving.

"*Bon Voyage*, dear boy!" she called out.

Chapter 8

Onlee One was thrown into a hold and locked in. The engines wound up to full throttle. They were on their way... but where to?

He looked round the gloomy hold. A faint but familiar smell wafted through the air-vent. He sniffed again.

Ratuschka!

Onlee One wasn't a Champion Tunnel Mazer for nothing. He soon had the grille off and was squeezing his way through the air system, towards the cockpit.

There she was. He could see her talking to Dark Claw, who was on a video screen.

"We have him, Dark Claw," she announced. "But I'm afraid our price has gone up. If you still want Onlee One, you'll have to pay twice as much as we agreed."

Dark Claw roared with anger.

"You have some nerve, Ratuschka. I show no mercy to those who cross me!" He slammed his paw down on the desk in front of him and the screen blacked out.

Ratuschka smiled. "He wants Onlee One more than anything else," she said. "He'll pay up." The other rats didn't look so sure.

The Pi-rats sat in silence, waiting to see what Dark Claw would do. It wasn't long before they found out.

"Now we're for it!" shouted one of the gang. "Look at the screen…Robo Kats heading this way. There's loads of them…we don't stand a chance!

Ratuschka shouted over the noise of panic.

We're perfectly safe. Dark Claw wants Onlee One alive.

But the rest of the gang weren't going to wait to find out. They ran to the escape pods.

Airlocks hissed and the escape pods blasted themselves away from the ship.

Onlee One was left all alone in the eerie silence.

Kicking out the grille, he lowered himself down to the cockpit. The video came alive. Dark Claw filled the screen.

"You!" he gasped. "Where is Ratuschka?"

Onlee One ignored him as he worked out the ship's controls.

"Where is Ratuschka?" bellowed Dark Claw.

Finally, Onlee One looked up at the screen.

"She's gone," he said. "Just like I'm about to do!"

He eased the control stick forward. The engines roared into full throttle. The power thrust him back into his seat, making it harder for him to set a course. Not that it mattered, any course would do.

"I'm out of here!" he called to the fading image of Dark Claw!

Chapter 9

The Robo Kats did not open fire.

"Dark Claw really does want me alive," thought Onlee One.

He checked his position on the star
chart and decided to land on a small
planet close by. He needed to hide out
for a while. Two Robo Kat ships were
still on his tail

Onlee One swept down into the planet's bright pink atmosphere. Two Robo Kat ships were still on his tail. He set his ship on autopilot and climbed into the last escape pod.

He came in low over the purple sea and waited until he saw land before pulling the ejector handle.

Just before his pod hit the water, Onlee One saw his ship land automatically on the beach. At least he'd have a way to get back off the planet.

His escape pod crashed into the waves and plunged deep underwater. Then, slowly, it rose back to the surface.

The Robo Kat ships hovered over the beach for a while before they gave up searching for him. With a loud blast of their engines, they headed off into space.

Onlee One felt very lonely – as though he was the only life on the planet!

"What am I going to do now?" he whispered to himself.

Chapter 10

On Dark Moon, the metallic voice of a Robo Kat made a radio report.

"All escape pods have been destroyed. Ratuschka and her crew have been dealt with."

Another report echoed across the control room. It was the Robo Kat captain that had chased Onlee One to the planet.

We are on the planet and have searched the ship. It landed on autopilot. We have been tricked. Onlee One is not on board.

Dark Claw roared with rage.

It cannot be! I will have him!
I will have my revenge!

Have you seen the Dark Claw Website?

www.dark-claw.co.uk

Shoo Rayner designed and built the Dark Claw Website
himself, while he was writing the Dark Claw stories.
It is packed full of games and background stories about the
worlds of Onlee One, his friends and his enemies!

Why is Dark Claw so angry?
Why does he want to destroy the Muss?

 Where in the Universe is the planet Muss?
What is Litterbox? What is Kimono?

What is it like at the Tan Monastery School?
Why do the beds squeak?

All this and more. If you're a Dark Claw fan, you'll love the
Dark Claw website. It's all part of the story!

If you enjoyed this book you'll want to read
the other books in the Dark Claw Saga.

Tunnel Mazers
0 340 81754 2
The one with the very
smelly cheese!

Road Rage
0 340 81755 0
The one with the cool
racing machines!

Rat Trap
0 340 81756 9
The one with invisible
space ships!

Breakout!
0 340 81757 7
The one with nowhere
left to go!

The Guiding Paw
0 340 81758 5
The one with the Muss-
eating jellyfish!

The Black Hole
0 340 81759 3
The one with the end
of the story!

Find out more about Shoo Rayner and his other
fantastic books at www.shoo-rayner.co.uk

If you enjoyed this book you'll love these otherbooks by Shoo Rayner and Hodder Children's Books

The Rex Files
(Seriously weird!)

0 340 71432 8   The Life-Snatcher
0 340 71466 2   The Phantom Bantam
0 340 71467 0   The Bermuda Triangle
0 340 71468 9   The Shredder
0 340 71469 7   The Frightened Forest
0 340 71470 0   The Baa-Baa Club

Or what about the wonderful
Ginger Ninja?

0 340 61955 4   The Ginger Ninja
0 340 61956 2   The Return of Tiddles
0 340 61957 0   The Dance of the Apple Dumplings
0 340 61958 9   St Felix for the Cup
0 340 69379 7   World Cup Winners
0 340 69380 0   Three's a Crowd

And don't forget SUPERDAD!
(He's a bit soft really!)

0 7500 2694 4   Superdad
0 7500 2706 1   Superdad the SuperHero

Phone 012345 400414 and have a credit card ready

Please allow the following for postage and packing:
UK & BFPO – £1.00 for the first book, 50p for the second book, and 30p for each additional book ordered up to a maximum charge of £3.00.
OVERSEAS & EIRE – £2.00 for the first book, £1.00 for the second book, and 50p for each additional book.